DANNY ORLIS
AND HIS
BIG CHANCE

DANNY ORLIS
AND HIS
BIG CHANCE

BERNARD PALMER

ANEKO PRESS

Please note that several books in the Danny Orlis series are published by Sword of the Lord Publications and are available for purchase on their website, www.swordbooks.com.

Aneko Press *Youth*

www.anekopress.com

Aneko Press, Life Sentence Publishing, and our logos are trademarks of Life Sentence Publishing, Inc.
203 E. Birch Street
P.O. Box 652
Abbotsford, WI 54405

JUVENILE FICTION / Religious / Christian / Action & Adventure
Paperback ISBN: 978-1-62245-976-6
eBook ISBN: 978-1-62245-977-3
10 9 8 7 6 5 4 3 2 1
Available where books are sold

CONTENTS

CHAPTER 1

POST OFFICE ROBBERY

Danny Orlis got up at his usual time that Sunday morning and looked outdoors. A sharp fall wind was ripping the last remnants of leaves from the oak and maple in the front yard, and swirling long spirals of dirt across the pavement.

He got his Bible from its place on the dresser and went downstairs. There was just time enough to go over the lesson again before Sunday school. But when he got downstairs there was a note on the living room table saying that Mr. and Mrs. Meyer had to be away for the day.

"Would you please fix breakfast for Karen and Kirk, Danny?" Mrs. Meyer had written. "And wake them up in time to get to Sunday school?"

He cooked cereal, as he often did at home, made toast, and fried eggs before going to the stairway to call the two children. Karen came down dressed for

Sunday school, but Kirk came into the kitchen wearing the tops of his pajamas and a pair of dirty jeans. He was carrying a stack of comic books.

"Boy, you don't look like you're ready for Sunday school," Danny said, smiling.

"I don't think I'm going this morning," Kirk replied disinterestedly.

"And what's bringing this on?" asked Danny.

"I just don't want to go this morning. It's always the same old thing. I won't miss it very much." And Kirk sat down at the table and opened his comic books. "Besides, I'm going to stay at home and read these. I've got to give them back to a kid tomorrow."

Danny pulled up a chair and sat down at the table across from him.

"Do you think you're doing what God wants you to do, Kirk?" he asked quietly.

The boy didn't answer.

"Do you think it's better for you to stay home from Sunday school to read comics than it is for you to go to God's house?"

Kirk looked up. "You're just making it into something," he retorted defensively. "It's not as bad as all that. I'm just going to stay home this one Sunday, that's all."

"That's one of the ways Satan works, fella," Danny said. "He deceives us into thinking that it will be all right to go against God's wishes 'just this once.' After we've done that it's so much easier to get us to do it again and again, until he's gotten us completely out of God's will."

"Quit preaching at me, will you?" Kirk snapped. "I'm just going to stay home this once, that's all. I've got to read these comics before I have to give them back."

Danny picked up one of the crime comics on the top of the pile and would have looked at it, but Kirk snatched it from him, slammed it back on the pile, and turned back to the one he was reading.

* * * *

Danny had some studying to do that night and he hurried home after church to get at it. Mr. and Mrs. Meyer hadn't returned yet.

He was sitting at the kitchen table reading American History and eating a piece of cake when the door opened and Kirk came in, his arms loaded with comics.

"Hi, fella," Danny said to him pleasantly.

Kirk grunted and hurried past.

"Don't you want a piece of cake before you go to bed?" Danny called to him. "There's plenty of it here."

The younger boy stood there hesitantly.

"Better have some," urged Danny.

"I–I think I'd better get up to bed." Ever since Danny spoke to him about spending so much time reading comics, Kirk had been avoiding him.

The Orlis boy stared after him.

The next morning on the way to school Rick Haines hurried to catch up with Danny.

"Did you hear about all the excitement last night?" he asked, panting.

"I didn't know we ever had any excitement in Cedarton," answered Danny.

"I'm not fooling," Rick retorted. "We had some big excitement here last night. Somebody robbed the post office."

"The post office?" Danny echoed. "Are you sure? When did it happen?"

"Between 8:30 and 9:30, as nearly as they can figure. The men noticed it when they went down to work the mail for the 10 o'clock train."

The two boys walked together in silence.

"And the strange thing is," Rick continued, "my dad heard that just last week a new comic came into the corner store. It showed some guys robbing a post office. And this robbery was done exactly the same way."

"But surely no one would read a comic book and then go out and rob the post office. That doesn't seem possible," Danny interrupted.

"The sheriff thinks that it happened that way," Rick insisted. "He said that this comic showed exactly how the guys went into the post office and everything. Whoever robbed our post office did everything in exactly the same way as it was shown in that comic. It's serious enough so the authorities are going to check all the comic book customers and find those who have that particular comic."

Danny Orlis stopped short. Suddenly he remembered the last comic of Kirk's that he had seen. He could still see the cover! Two men were slipping out of the window of a big gray building, while a third was shooting a police officer.

"The Post-Office Gang!" He could still recall those bold red letters across the top.

The sheriff was going to question every boy who had one of those comics. And Kirk Meyer was one of them!

A strange look must have come over Danny's face, for Rick laughed at him.

"What's the matter? You aren't afraid that they'll find out you've been buying comics, are you?" asked Rick.

"No," Danny answered, shaking his head slowly. "I haven't been buying any comics. But I know someone who has."

They walked across the street in silence.

"I used to think that you were pretty narrow and straight-laced for not liking it when Kirk and the other kids read comics," Rick continued. "But I can see now why you feel that way about them."

Danny did not answer him. His mind was still on Kirk Meyer.

The kids at school were all talking about the post office robbery as the two boys walked up the steps of the building and went inside.

Danny Orlis went directly to the library and got a history book to use for research. He had to have that paper finished and handed in by the end of the week. Still, he found it difficult to study. Kirk had had a copy of that comic. And he had been out until almost 10 o'clock the night before. What if—? He did not dare to even allow himself to think about it.

When he got home from school that day Kirk was already there, sitting alone in the living room.

"Hi, Danny!"

The Orlis boy crossed over to the big easy chair in the opposite corner and sat down.

"You're home from school a little early, aren't you, Kirk?" He tried to speak pleasantly, but his voice had an odd, insistent tone.

"I just didn't feel like hanging around school today," Kirk replied. "I get enough of that place when we're in class."

There was a long silence.

It hadn't been that way the week before. Kirk had lingered in the hall with the rest of the kids, talking and laughing excitedly.

Once or twice the younger boy looked up at Danny as though to speak. Then he turned quickly away and leafed through the book on his lap.

"D-D-Danny?" he spoke at last.

The older boy put aside his paper and looked up. "Yes?"

"Danny, they–they won't be questioning everyone who bought one of those Post-Office Gang comics, will they?" His voice was insistent. "Will they?"

"Rick said the sheriff told his dad that was what

they planned to do," Danny answered. "He said that the post office here was robbed in the same way as the one that was robbed in the comic book, so they were sure that there was some connection. Of course, they'll check fingerprints and all that sort of thing. They always do. But they're going to get to the bottom of this comic book affair too. They think it provides a real lead."

Kirk's face went pale, and he began to bite his lower lip nervously.

"But it isn't against the law to buy comics," the boy protested. "They can't do anything to a guy for that, can they?"

Danny shook his head.

"No, there isn't any law against buying comics. The comic is just one piece of evidence. But if a guy bought one, he may have to prove where he was last night at the time the robbery was committed. The police will certainly talk to him."

Kirk started to read his book again, restlessly. His eyes scanned the page, but every now and then he looked up.

"Danny," he blurted out suddenly, "can they find out who bought that comic? For sure, I mean? They've got a whole rack of them. And there are three or four girls who sell them. They couldn't find out the name of everyone who–who happened to buy one of those comics, could they?"

"It might be a little hard," Danny answered. "But

they've got a good idea of the names of the regular comic book customers. That will give them a start. From what I've heard they just keep working on a thing like that until they get to the bottom of it. And they don't care how long it takes. You see, robbing a post office is a federal crime, and the FBI takes over."

Kirk winced and ran his fingers through his dark hair.

"I don't see how they could find everyone who bought that comic book," he said. "They'd surely miss a few."

Danny crossed his legs and leaned back in the chair.

"I don't think they'll be missing anyone," he answered. "In the first place the girls will remember the names of a few who bought it. Some of the kids will remember seeing guys with it, or hearing them talk about it. That will make the list a little longer. And then, like I said, they might just get the names of the ones who regularly buy comics and start checking them, one by one." He shook his head. "No, I don't think they'll miss anyone by the time they finish their investigation."

Kirk swallowed hard.

"But why are they so interested in that comic anyway?" he stammered. "I don't think it had anything to do with what happened."

"That isn't what the authorities say, Kirk," Danny said. "And you know they've been checking into things like that for a long, long time. The wrong kind of comics can cause a guy to think that he might be able to pull off a robbery like this post office thing and get away with it."

Kirk Meyer got up quickly when Danny finished speaking and hurried from the room.

The Orlis boy sat for a long while staring across the living room. Then he got up and walked over to the fireplace. Why he did it he didn't exactly know. But he stooped and picked up a piece of charred paper that had fallen out of the grate. He examined it absent-mindedly.

Danny caught his breath. It was the corner of a comic book cover. He recognized it in an instant. Kirk had burned his copy of the Post-Office Gang comic!

Danny straightened slowly. Why was Kirk so frightened? His own heart chilled.

CHAPTER 2

A VISIT FROM THE SHERIFF

That night at the supper table Kirk Meyer was unusually quiet. The others were laughing and talking excitedly after a day apart, but he ate in silence, staring down at his plate.

"I've got some news for you," Mr. Meyer said abruptly, "that I'm sure you'll all be happy to hear."

Kirk looked up quickly, concern in his eyes. He colored slightly as he saw that Danny Orlis was watching him.

"Yes," his dad went on, "I picked up Harold Forester this morning. Took him to the depot so he could catch the morning train to Minneapolis. He told me that he's a Christian now. He's taken Christ as his personal Savior."

"Oh, isn't that wonderful!" Mrs. Meyer exclaimed happily. She was silent momentarily. "I wonder what Mrs. Forester will do now?"

"What do you mean?" asked her husband.

"She's been so terribly disturbed since Marilyn became a Christian. She's trying every way possible to get her to do the things the Country Club set does. I just wonder how she'll be with two Christians in the family."

"I asked Harold how she was taking it," Mr. Meyer said, "but he only shook his head."

"She must not be so terribly mad at her now, Mom," Karen put in. "I saw the two of them in the store after school today. Marilyn was trying on dresses and suits and everything."

"Maybe she's going to send her away to that private school after all," Danny suggested. "Marilyn told us that her mom kept talking about all the new clothes she could get if she did go there."

"She surely wouldn't send her away now," Mrs. Meyer replied.

When evening devotions were over, Danny called Kay and made arrangements to meet her at about 7:30.

When he got to the corner store a few minutes early she was already there, sitting in a booth with Marilyn and Tim.

"Hi!" he said, walking up to them and sliding into the booth beside Kay. "What's going on? What's new?"

"I was just telling Kay and Tim that I can't understand what's come over Mom," Marilyn replied. "'This morning she was so furious that she would hardly speak to me. Accused me of wrecking her life, and Daddy's too. I don't know what took place, or why, but when I got out of school this afternoon, she was waiting for me. She took me down to the store and told me to buy all the new clothes I wanted."

"Wonderful!" Kay exclaimed. She tried to keep the envy from her voice, but in spite of herself, it crept in.

"She told me that she thought I must have been planning on all those lovely clothes she had promised I could have if I went away to school," Marilyn continued. "And now that she and Daddy had decided I wasn't going she wanted me to have the clothes anyway." Marilyn shook her head. "I can't understand it."

"You don't suppose that she's been thinking about the fact that your dad has accepted Christ; and you're a Christian, and she wants to accept the Lord too?" Kay suggested.

"Oh, I hope so! But I don't know. All I can tell you is that she bought me the loveliest dresses you ever saw. And she told me that if I wanted to get a new fur jacket after Daddy got back that she thought she could talk him into it."

Kay looked at her wistfully.

"I always wanted a fur coat or jacket," she said. "But I don't suppose I'll ever get the chance. I'll do well to get a new cloth coat this year."

"Oh," the other girl replied carelessly, "I had one fur coat, but it was just a cheap one. I don't think it cost more than $300.00."

"Three hundred dollars!" Danny exclaimed. "What kind of a coat was that?"

"Muskrat."

"Do you mean to tell me that you paid that much for a coat made out of those skinny little rats I trap in the wintertime?" asked Danny. "I'll bet the muskrat doesn't know he's wearing such an expensive coat. If he did, he'd probably shake out of it and sell it himself."

"I wish I had half that much money," Tim said, only half-jokingly. "I've got to get some shoes and winter clothes and a coat. And the worst of it is that I don't know where it's coming from. Mom doesn't have it to spare."

The smile fled from Marilyn's face. She flushed deeply, and for an instant or two all were silent.

"I'm sorry, Tim," she said haltingly.

"Oh, don't worry about me," he told her brightly. "I'm going to get a job one of these days. Then I can buy myself a fur coat."

The girls laughed at that, but Danny Orlis saw the hurt look in his friend's eyes.

The group sat there for a few minutes talking about other things, but the conversation was strained.

* * * *

Danny Orlis didn't see Kirk that night when he got home. And in the morning, he got up, ate breakfast hurriedly, and rushed to school to cram for an English test. So he didn't get to see the younger boy until school was out that afternoon.

Danny had been so busy all day that he hadn't thought about the post office robbery at all until he got home and saw Kirk sitting in the living room. The boy's face was pale and his hands were trembling.

"What's the matter?" Danny asked. "What's wrong?"

Kirk looked up, and Danny could see the sweat on the boy's forehead.

"You–you know about that comic book and the post office," Kirk said, stammering.

Danny nodded.

"Well, the sheriff and another guy were here to see me a little while ago," Kirk stammered. "They found out that I had bought one of those comics and they wanted to know where I'd been that Sunday night when–when the post office was robbed."

"Well, you could tell them, couldn't you?" Danny asked. He spoke confidently, but his heart skipped a beat as he saw the look on Kirk's face.

"Danny," he said, "when the sheriff was here I–I lied to him!"

CHAPTER 3

AT THE SHERIFF'S HOUSE

Danny Orlis and Kirk stared at each other.

"You don't mean that, do you, Kirk?"

The younger boy nodded miserably. "I just couldn't do any differently."

Danny put his arm about Kirk's shoulder and walked with him across the room to the sofa where they sat down together. Kirk cleared his throat but did not speak.

"Why don't you tell me what this is all about?" Danny pleaded.

Kirk looked up at him. The hurt was deep in his eyes and his lips trembled uncertainly.

"I can't, Danny. I can't tell you a thing."

"You're known as a Christian here in Cedarton," Danny began slowly. "That means that you've got an obligation to be truthful and honorable at all times, regardless of how hard it is."

Kirk fumbled for his handkerchief. "What'll they do to me, Danny?" he cried. "When they find out that I've lied to them?"

"It's bad enough to lie to anyone," Danny Orlis answered. "It's a mighty serious thing to lie to an officer of the law."

"I wish I'd never seen a comic," Kirk blurted out. "I wish I'd listened to you and never even looked at one." With that, he jumped to his feet and fled upstairs.

Danny Orlis watched him go. A strange, gnawing pain grasped at his heart. He started up to Kirk's room, then stopped uncertainly and for a moment or two stood on the staircase, indecision furrowing his face.

Kirk's door was locked when he tried it.

"Kirk," he whispered, knocking lightly. "Kirk, it's me, Danny. Won't you let me come in for a couple of minutes?"

There was no answer.

"I'd like to talk to you," Danny pleaded.

He stood there, praying that the boy would unlock the door, but he did not. Finally, Danny went to his own room.

Kirk was in trouble – great trouble. And there wasn't a thing he would let Danny or anyone else do for him.

Danny sat down beside the bed for a long while, fingering his Bible thoughtfully. It was times like these when he needed his dad. If only he could talk things over with him. He'd know what to do.

Danny laid his Bible carefully on the bed and knelt as he had seen his dad do so many times when he was faced with things that troubled him.

"O Lord Jesus," he began to pray, "You know about this post office robbery and the way Kirk is involved. You know how he sinned by lying to the sheriff. You know how deeply he's involved. Just guide him and help him to do what is right. Help him to see that he's got to go to the sheriff and tell him the truth. Speak to his heart...."

For a long while after he finished Danny continued to kneel beside the bed. Then he got up and went down to the kitchen table and began to study.

As he went downstairs, Kirk, who had been lying across his bed, raised up on one elbow, listening. He had heard Danny come to the door and knock. He should have let him in. He really wanted to talk to him. He had to talk to somebody. Now he sat up on the bed and brushed his hand nervously across his face.

But he knew already what Danny would say. And he couldn't go to the sheriff. He couldn't tell him that he had lied and ask for forgiveness.

Kirk stared at the rumpled bedspread, without actually seeing it.

He heard the front door open, and someone came up the stairs, but he did not move. If only he had taken Danny's advice and had gotten rid of those old comics! If only he hadn't let reading them crowd the Bible reading and daily devotions out of his life! Slowly, miserably, he slipped to his knees beside the bed and tried to pray.

"O heavenly Father," he began, "be with me and watch over me and help me—." He stopped suddenly. How could he ask God to help him when he had deliberately lied to the sheriff? How could he expect God to hear his prayer when he had sinned so terribly?

Kirk gulped hard. And, rubbing at his eyes with his fists, he stumbled to his feet.

The window shade was up and in the growing darkness he could see that it had started to snow. Soft, white flakes were drifting down to the sidewalk and the browned grass below. It was late in the season, and snow was long past due. He had seen blizzards start that same way, so stealthily that before one realized what was happening, the rising wind was choked with snow.

That was the way a lie sneaked up on a guy. First, you slipped away from God just a little. And then—. He bit his lip nervously, as though to bite the torment from his mind.

The wind came up a little, even as he watched. It snatched the newly fallen snow from its resting place and whisked it across the ground.

In the house across the street the family was decorating a Christmas tree.

Gene Parker, who lived there, was standing on a

ladder to put a snow-white star on the tip of the tree. Mr. Parker was painting a verse in watercolors on their huge picture window. "For God so loved the world, that he gave his only begotten Son—."

Kirk Meyer swallowed hard. What could Christmas mean to him this year?

He walked back to his dresser and picked up his Testament.

His sister Karen came to the head of the stairs just then and called him to supper.

"I don't feel like eating," he told her.

Then, because he knew that his mom would be up to see what was the matter with him if he didn't go down to eat, he opened the door and walked slowly down to the dining room.

Danny looked at him quizzically. But Kirk avoided his steady glance. He kept his eyes glued to his plate all through dinner. And as soon as he finished eating he got up and started to leave the room.

"Kirk," his dad said to him, "aren't you forgetting something?"

He turned back quickly. "What's that?"

"We haven't had our devotions yet."

Kirk gritted his teeth as they prayed after the Bible reading. He was certain that his face must be flaming, and that his heart was beating so loudly that all the rest of them could hear it. However, if any of them noticed anything wrong, they did not say anything about it.

Kirk had a great deal of studying to do that night. But try as he would, he could not keep his mind on his lessons. Every time he opened his book, he could see the lurid cover of the Post-Office Gang Comic before him. Every time he looked up, he could see the accusing gaze of the sheriff.

The officer thought he had told the truth. Kirk knew that the officer had taken it for granted, because Kirk was a Christian and had fine parents. Nobody would ever know. Nobody, that is, except Danny. And he wouldn't tell. Kirk straightened suddenly. Or would he?

Danny Orlis was up in his room now, getting ready to go somewhere. Perhaps he was going to see the sheriff. Perhaps he would tell him about the lie. Panic seized Kirk, and for an instant or two it held him in its grip.

But of course, Danny wouldn't tell on him, he reasoned. Danny was a good friend of his.

Kirk turned back to his books, but the print was blurred before his eyes. Regardless of whether the sheriff ever learned of it or not, Kirk had lied to him. He had told him things that weren't true. Suddenly he pushed back from his desk and got to his feet. He knew now what he had to do.

He went timidly down the hall to Danny's room where the Orlis boy was just finishing dressing.

"Danny," he managed, "would–would you do something for me?"

"Certainly, Kirk."

"I–I'm going over to see the sheriff," he stammered. "And I–I'd like to have you go with me."

They got into their heavy coats and together they walked out into the cold and snow.

"I–I'm scared," Kirk said weakly. "What do you think he'll do to me?"

The sheriff came to the door in answer to their knock and showed them into the living room.

"Now what is it that you want to see me about," he began cordially.

For an instant or two Kirk wavered, chewing desperately on his lips.

"I don't know how to begin," he said, stammering. "But I–I didn't tell you the truth today when you were talking to me about that comic and the post office robbery."

If the sheriff was surprised, he gave no sign. He waited until Kirk could continue.

"I–I didn't have anything to do with it myself," he said at last. "But a bunch of us were talking about robbing the post office after we read the comic. We didn't mean it at all. We were just talking for fun, but a couple of the kids seemed to be awfully interested all of a sudden. They borrowed the comic and took it home with them."

"Go on," said the sheriff calmly.

"That was the day before the post office was robbed," Kirk continued. Then he leaned forward and lowered his voice. "And the day after the robbery I happened to come up behind those kids in the corridor at school. And I saw them looking at a big roll of money!"

"Are you sure of that, Kirk?" the law enforcement officer demanded. "That's a serious charge."

"I–I should have told you about it before, but I was scared. I–I didn't want to say anything to anyone about it," Kirk confessed.

The sheriff got up quickly. "I want to get those names," he said. "This sounds like the break we've been looking for."

"I–I'm awfully sorry that I lied to you," Kirk told him.

"Sometimes we all do things that we shouldn't do," the sheriff answered, slipping into his coat. "The important thing is that we realize that we've done wrong, and that we ought to do the best we can to make it right and to see that it doesn't happen again."

"But there's one thing I never can make right," Kirk went on miserably. "That comic was mine. I let those kids read it. I'm really the one who's to blame."

"I wouldn't say that it was entirely your fault," the officer told him. "Those boys had to have the wrong ideas and the wrong slant on life even to think about doing a thing like this. But when it comes to a matter like these comic books, I don't believe we think enough about what harm they can do. I've seen enough of it in my job the past three years that I've been sheriff to know what terrible things they can cause."

The sheriff was in a hurry to get out and see the boys Kirk had told him about. So Danny and Kirk walked home in the drifting snow.

"Feel better now?" the Orlis boy asked him.

"A little," Kirk said. "But I still can't get over what I did. I should have listened to you the first time, when you told me that comics were taking me away from reading the Bible, and having devotions, and keeping me from going to Sunday school and church. I should have listened to you, Danny. Then this awful thing might not have happened."

The Orlis boy nodded.

"That's right," he said. "But you know the wonderful thing about it all is that if we are truly repentant for what we've done, and with God's help aren't going to let it happen again, the matter is over and done with. The book is closed."

Kirk smiled warmly for the first time in days.

"I've learned my lesson," he said firmly. "I'm never going to let anything else keep me from Bible reading and prayer again. That's when a guy gets in trouble. When he starts to neglect those things."

CHAPTER 4

SHARING CHRISTMAS

Thursday evening before Christmas, school was dismissed for the holidays. The teachers had already packed their bags and were rushing off to their homes. But Danny Orlis and Kay were sitting in a booth at the drugstore. They ordered some hot chocolate and looked anxiously out the window at the fine, wind-driven snow that had begun to fall again within the past hour.

"It's snowing again," Kay said anxiously.

Danny nodded.

Kay slowly sipped her hot drink and glanced up at the frost-etched window once more to catch a glimpse of the weather outside.

"Honestly, I don't know what I'd do this Christmas if your parents hadn't asked me to come back to the Angle with you for the holidays. When we're busy at school and church it doesn't seem so lonesome, but it's the holidays when I miss Mom the most and—." Kay's voice trailed away, and Danny thought he saw her lower lip tremble a little.

Danny nodded sympathetically. He knew what it must be like to be away from his parents at Christmas time. He knew how he felt now as he looked out and watched the clouds, and hoped and prayed that it wouldn't storm enough to keep them from getting up to the Northwest Angle.

"I don't think I could stand it," the girl continued, "if it weren't for the fact that I know Mom is in God's will and helping win souls for Him. And that the same God who is taking care of her is taking care of me too."

Kirk Meyer and a friend came into the corner store just then, stomping the snow from their feet and brushing their coats. The other boy went directly over to the counter where the comics were kept and picked one up. Kirk joined him and talked with him for a moment or two. Then Kirk took the comic from the other boy and put it back on the counter.

"I don't think we're going to have to worry about Kirk reading comics anymore, Kay," whispered Danny.

"I'm so happy," she said. "And I'm glad that other affair turned out all right too. I was afraid that Kirk might be involved in it in some way when you told me that he had lied to the sheriff."

"No," Danny answered. "The sheriff went out to see the boys. They confessed everything. Kirk didn't have a thing to do with it, but the kids did get the idea from his comic."

"What time tomorrow do you think Tex will be here?" Kay asked at last, ignoring the snow, and the warnings of a blizzard.

"Mrs. Williams will probably phone us when he leaves Baudette," Danny replied. "That'll give us time enough to get out to the airport to meet him."

They finished their hot chocolate and sat for a time talking before Kay looked at her watch.

"I didn't realize it was so late," she said, getting to her feet. "I've got to run. I promised Marilyn that I'd go to prayer meeting with her tonight."

"I'll walk over there with you," Danny told her, helping her into her coat. "I'd been planning on missing prayer meeting tonight so I could get my bags packed. But I guess I can get my stuff together when I get home."

* * * *

It was still snowing when they left the church after the prayer meeting. A fine, soft snow was falling that would pile into towering drifts at the faintest suggestion of wind. And it was still snowing when Danny got his suitcase packed and went to bed that night. And, when he awakened sometime before midnight and raised on one elbow to look out, the snow was still sifting down. However, the following day dawned bright and clear. The wind had swept the clouds away during the night. And, although it was bitter cold, the sun shone brightly on the blanket of white.

Kirk was just going down to breakfast as Danny came out of his room.

"Hi!" the Orlis boy said. "It certainly looks as though the Lord answered our prayers for good flying weather today."

Kirk grinned. That warm, friendly feeling between them was back again.

Tex Williams landed at the Cedarton airport at about 10:00. Danny and Kay were already there, waiting. And before noon they were circling the Orlis cabin.

"Look!" Danny exclaimed, pointing excitedly. "They're all out to meet us!"

"I thought you'd never get here," Roxie said when they touched down. "Ron's got the Christmas tree all picked out. We've got to decorate it and everything."

Danny looked about. "Speaking of Ron," he said, "where is the guy anyway? I thought everyone was out here to see us come in."

"He went out to look at his traps this morning," Mr. Orlis said. "He should have been back half an hour ago. I suppose he ran into something that delayed him."

"Well, we wouldn't go for the Christmas tree until after dinner anyway," Danny said. "And I'm about starved."

"Everything's on the table waiting for you, Danny," his mom broke in.

They had finished eating when Ron came hurrying in. He shouted a word of greeting to Danny and Kay, stomping the snow from his boots and pulling off his heavy leather mittens.

"I stopped over to see how Mr. Beecher is," he explained. "His wife's our teacher, Danny."

"Is Mr. Beecher sick?" asked Mrs. Orlis.

"Didn't you know, Mom?" Ron continued. "He was working in the woods yesterday and a log fell on his foot. His leg swelled up pretty much. Mrs. Beecher had to go home during recess yesterday and see how he was."

"Have they taken him to the doctor?" questioned his mom.

"No, but Mrs. Dawson came over and dressed his foot," Ron said, sighing deeply. "But it's not going to be much of a merry Christmas around their place this year."

"What do you mean?" Kay put in.

"They were going down to Warroad to be with some of their folks," Ron said. "They'd made arrangements to fly back with Tex today. Now they can't go. And they don't even have any of their presents up here. It's sure not going to be much of a Christmas for them."

There was a long silence.

"That's too bad," Carl Orlis said after a time. "They've had a hard time anyway."

"Maybe we could have them over here tonight," Roxie suggested. "We've always got room for somebody extra. And I've got that scarf Aunt Mabel sent me. I could give it to Mrs. Beecher. And maybe someone else could find something to give to Mr. Beecher. They could celebrate Christmas with us."

Ron shook his head. "That's out," he said firmly. "Mr. Beecher can't go anywhere. That leg of his is too bad."

"It's a shame that they're going to have to be alone, and on Christmas too," sighed Mrs. Orlis.

Carl Orlis put down his fork and looked over at his wife. "You know I think Roxie is the one who has the idea."

"But, Dad," Ron broke in, "Mr. Beecher isn't able to go anywhere."

"But there's no reason why we can't go over there," his dad answered.

"Do you mean that we should have our Christmas over there?" Roxie asked, in surprise.

Ron's face clouded.

"But, Dad," he protested, "we've never spent a Christmas away from here since we came to the Angle to live with you and Mom. It wouldn't seem like Christmas at all if we weren't here at the cabin for Christmas Eve."

There was a long silence.

Then Mrs. Orlis laid her hand on Ron's arm. "What sort of Christmas do you think the Beechers will have if they're over there all alone?" she asked in a soft voice.

Ron Orlis swallowed hard.

"I've got a couple of things in my suitcase that I can give to Mr. Beecher," Danny said, pushing back from the table.

"And I've got a new billfold I'd like to give him," Ron offered, brightening. And then he smiled. "I think this is going to be lots of fun."

Hurriedly they got out the gifts for the Beechers and wrapped them. Kay and Mrs. Orlis fixed a chicken, baked a cake, and made some ice cream, while Danny and Ron went out and cut two small Christmas trees and brought them in.

"One is for the Beechers," Ron explained. "We figured that if we got two small trees we'd have decorations enough for both of them."

* * * *

"I don't know how we can ever thank you," Mr. Beecher said from his bed, after they had finished the dinner. The twins and Danny and Kay were busy decorating the tree. "I don't mind telling you that we were looking forward to a mighty bleak Christmas around here."

"And instead," his wife put in quickly, "this has been one of the best Christmases we've ever had."

When they finished decorating the tree, Mr. Beecher turned to his wife.

"Mabel," he said, "why don't you get that Bible off the dresser? I think it would be nice to have Carl read the Christmas story this evening."

Slowly Carl Orlis opened the Bible to the Book of Luke and began to read: " 'For unto you is born this day in the city of David a savior, which is Christ the Lord. And this shall be a sign unto you; Ye shall find the babe wrapped in swaddling clothes, lying in a manger....'"

CHAPTER 5

BUSY HOLIDAYS

It was bitter cold on the Northwest Angle of Minnesota during the Christmas holidays. For two or three days the threat of a raging blizzard was in the air. Dull gray clouds stretched from sky to sky. Every now and then violent snow flurries whipped across the frozen lake in the teeth of a chill wind.

"It looks as though that blizzard we've been expecting for the past two or three weeks is about here," Carl Orlis said to Danny, as the two of them chopped wood for the heating stove.

"I'm glad it held off as long as it did. If it had come a week ago, Kay and I wouldn't have been able to get here for Christmas."

"I don't suppose it matters so much whether you get back to school on time or not," his dad said, laughing.

Danny laid aside his ax and stooped to load his arms with firewood.

"I certainly hope that Tex got back home all right. It looked bad about the time he took off after dinner."

"He ought to be home by now," said Mr. Orlis.

Together they filled the woodbox on the back porch and went into the kitchen to take off their boots and heavy clothes. Danny turned to his dad and said, "I've been wanting to talk with you about that airmail letter Tex brought me this morning, Dad."

Mr. Orlis looked up and asked, "The one that came from the university out west?"

Danny nodded.

"You remember the guy, don't you? He was up here fishing last summer. He was the one who talked to me about going to Westbrook University to play football."

"Yes, I remember him," Carl Orlis answered.

"They offered me a wonderful deal," Danny said, trying to keep the excitement out of his voice, but not succeeding very well. "They'll give me a football scholarship good for all four years, and a soft job at the school. He said that I wouldn't even have to work during the football season, but that I'd still be paid for it."

Danny's dad pulled off his fleece-lined boots and put on a pair of shoes.

"Well," he said at last, "I'll have to admit that does sound good. You know, Danny, the way things are, I may not be able to help you in college nearly as much as I'd like to."

"I know that," Danny replied. "And I surely don't want to be a burden on you either. But this way I could go to school, get an education, and play big-time football. And it wouldn't cost me a cent. Not a single cent."

"That's all very true," Mr. Orlis answered. "But that's really not the important thing, Danny. The important thing is whether it's the Lord's will for you or not." He was silent for a moment. "Tell me," he continued, "have you made it a matter of prayer?"

Danny looked up quickly.

"I've prayed about it a little," he said lamely. "But it seems to me that the reasonable thing to do is to take up the offer before they change their minds. A guy doesn't get a big chance like this every day."

"We can't rule the Lord out that easily, Danny," answered his dad as he put another stick of wood in the kitchen range and stirred up the fire.

"Your mother and I always hoped that you would go to a Bible school for a couple of years at least," he continued thoughtfully. "The most important thing in getting an education is for a young Christian to get himself thoroughly grounded in the Word of God."

"But Dad," Danny protested, "if I go to a Bible school, I won't get another chance to play football. Just think. Westbrook will let me play and pay my expenses too. I don't see how I can pass it up."

"The decision is yours," Mr. Orlis told him seriously. "But you can't think only of material things. There are eternal values to take into consideration too."

Danny was quiet.

"I know that, Dad," he said at last. "But I think that this is the way God is going to provide. He's given me this terrific opportunity. And with things as tough as they are financially, it looks to me as though this is His way of providing."

Carl Orlis said nothing.

For a long while Danny stared at the floor. All of reason was on his side. He had been going over the arguments all morning. And yet, what about the Lord's will for him? Where would God rather have him? He sighed deeply and, taking the letter from his pocket, he read it again. He was still reading it when Kay came in to talk to him.

The storm continued to threaten throughout the afternoon and evening but didn't quite come off. The mercury fell to 36° below, and the wind died down. But the clouds still hung in the air, spitting snow every now and then as though to keep reminding them what could happen.

The clouds were still threatening the next morning, but Danny, Kay, and the twins finished breakfast hurriedly, and set out on skis to run Ron's trap line.

"Remember what happened last year, Kay?" Danny asked. "When we went out to check Ron's traps?"

"If I'd thought about it before we left the house," she replied, shuddering, "I'd probably have stayed home."

It was cold that morning, but there was a hard crust on the snow, and they were able to move rapidly from one trap to the other. By the time they reached Harrison Creek, Ron had two minks and a fox. He was beaming.

"If I can do as well on the rest of the traps," he said, "we'll have an awfully good catch for today."

"I think you've already got your quota," Danny told him.

"That's the trouble with you. You don't know how good a trapper I am," Ron laughingly replied.

It was so bitterly cold that Kay and Roxie decided to go over to the Beecher cabin and wait while the boys checked the rest of the traps. Danny and Ron almost went on past the teacher's house, but at the last minute they decided to stop and see how Mr. Beecher was doing.

The schoolteacher met them at the door.

"Oh, I'm so glad to see you," she exclaimed excitedly. "I was just getting into my coat to start over to your place." Panic stood in her eyes.

"Is something wrong?" Danny asked.

She nodded significantly toward her husband who was lying on the bed in the other room. "We thought he was getting along all right," she whispered hoarsely, "but last night he took a turn for the worse. And this morning his fever is terribly high."

"Why don't we go and get Mrs. Dawson?" Danny asked, thinking of the registered nurse who made her home on the Angle.

"They've gone to Rosseau to spend Christmas and

they aren't back yet," Mrs. Beecher replied. "And I–I don't know what to do. I'm afraid Tom's got to have a doctor."

"Perhaps we can help," Kay offered.

Danny Orlis looked quickly up at the sky. It was beginning to snow again.

"Kay and Roxie can stay here and do what they can," Danny said. "Ron and I will beat it back home and radio for Tex to fly out and take Mr. Beecher down to the hospital."

For a brief instant, the teacher smiled her relief. "Do hurry, Danny," she said softly. "It looks as though it's going to storm and–and Tom's got to have a doctor." Her voice broke.

The two boys turned about and began to make their way over the snow. They pushed frantically toward their home on Pine Creek four miles away.

Danny Orlis looked anxiously up at the sky. Now that they were in such a hurry it looked as though it was going to storm at any moment. The clouds seemed to press down to the tops of the trees. A faint suggestion of wind rustled the bare branches. And a few hard flecks of snow hit their frost-whitened cheeks.

"If–if it storms, Tex won't be able to get up here, Danny," Ron said nervously. "Then what'll we do?"

"We've got to pray that he does get through," his brother told him.

They had taken the long way over to the Beecher cabin, without thought of time. But now they forced themselves over the hard crusted snow in almost a direct line toward the Orlis cabin. Neither Danny nor Ron mentioned the clouds again, but they both kept looking up anxiously. At last they made the cabin and told their parents what had happened.

"You get word to Tex by radio," Carl Orlis said to Danny. "I'll go over to Thompson's and borrow his air sled so we can get Mr. Beecher over here by the time Tex arrives."

"But why don't we have Tex go directly to Harrison Creek?" Danny asked.

"I don't think he can land over there."

Danny Orlis got one of the ham radio operators in Baudette on his radio, and by the time his dad got back with the air sled, the operator said that he had contacted Tex and the pilot would be on his way in an hour.

Mr. Orlis came to the door and called to Danny.

"Come on, fella," he shouted above the roar of the homemade air sled. "Do you know how to run this thing?"

"It's been quite a while, but I used to be able to."

"Then you boys get over to Harrison Creek and get Mr. Beecher here just as quickly as you can. I want to get some new markers on the landing strip for Tex. He almost hit a stump the last time he came in."

Danny and Ron climbed into the crudely built air sled and the older boy pulled back the throttle. The wind lashed their faces as they went racing toward the mouth of Pine Creek and cut sharply to the left to head for the Beecher cabin. Ron crouched low and shielded his face with his gloves.

The blast of frigid wind drove the cold to the very marrow of Danny's bones, but he did not slacken speed. He did not dare to. With Mr. Beecher's fever mounting they couldn't waste a minute. And at any time, the threatening blizzard could lash down upon them.

The Orlis boys sped down the narrow bay, almost at top speed, and turned into the mouth of Harrison Creek. Danny reached back to cut the throttle. As he did so the motor coughed spasmodically and died. He looked at his brother, who asked, "Why did you do that?"

"I didn't," Danny answered. "It just quit."

For an instant they stared at one another. And then, without warning, it began to snow again. This time there was no mistaking it. Fine, powdery snow went swirling along on the ice that stretched out ahead of them. There were a few flakes at first, dancing daintily along. But even as the two boys watched, the clouds unleashed their fury.

In an instant the very air was choked with snow.

CHAPTER 6

SNOWBOUND!

The swirling snow blotted out the Beecher cabin and the trees on either side of Harrison Creek. The wind awoke with a roar and was howling savagely through the tops of the barren trees. Danny and Ron Orlis were alone in a shroud of white.

"Do you think we can get the motor started?" Ron shouted above the roar of the storm.

"There isn't time to think about that now," Danny cried. "We've got to make it to that cabin as fast as we can!"

"Do–do you think we can find it?" Ron's lips were trembling with cold and fright.

"Take hold of my hand," his brother ordered sternly. "And whatever you do, don't let go!"

Together the two boys got out of the air sled and, stumbling through the howling blizzard, made their way toward the cabin.

"O Lord Jesus," Danny prayed inwardly, "help us to get to the Beecher cabin safely." He knew of all too many experienced men who had been caught out in a blizzard like this, only to flounder aimlessly in the snow.

The wind slacked for a moment or two, and Danny caught a glimpse of the big oak tree that marked the clearing where the Beecher cabin stood. It was only in sight for a moment, but that was enough. Danny tightened his grip on Ron's hand and headed straight for the big tree. The snow closed in about them in great, choking clouds, driving into their clothing and snatching their breath away. Danny's heart was pounding wildly as they stumbled off the ice, up the bank of the creek, and almost ran into the big tree.

"Let's stop here a minute," Danny shouted.

"But I'm awfully cold!" protested Ron.

"We've got to get our bearings. We can't take a chance on missing the house now!" the older boy continued.

In a moment or two the wind paused, as though to catch its breath. And for an instant the curtain settled back to give them a fleeting glimpse of the things around them.

"There's the cabin!" Ron shouted. "About a hundred yards away!"

Danny once more tightened his grip on Ron's hand, and they plunged forward. He didn't know how long it had taken them to make the few hundred yards from where they had left the stalled air sled to go to the Beecher cabin, nor how long they lay sprawled in exhaustion before the stove, after battling through the snow to the cabin door.

"Are you alright?" Kay asked anxiously.

Danny sat up slowly and looked about. "I–I think so," he said uncertainly.

"I didn't know that a guy could get so cold traveling such a short distance," Ron put in, rubbing his cheeks gingerly.

He would have said more, but Danny got to his feet. "How's Mr. Beecher?"

The woman started to cry again. Her eyes were red and swollen and her face was chalky white.

"He's not very good," Kay said softly. "Mrs. Beecher has been bathing him in cold water. I think his fever has gone down a little."

"But that red streak going up his leg," the teacher said. She spoke softly, tensely, as though all the strength had gone out of her. "There isn't anything we can do about that. And with the storm raging this way there isn't a chance for us to get him to a doctor."

Kay and Danny looked at each other.

"Don't talk that way," Kay told her. "We still have the Lord. He can undertake in a case like this."

"But Tom's got to have a doctor!" persisted the frightened woman.

Mr. Beecher was very ill. There was no question about that. Danny looked in the bedroom and saw that the injured man was lying with his eyes closed and his face red and feverish.

"If there were only something we could do about that infection," Kay whispered to Danny as they stood in the bedroom doorway.

"Mom has a remedy for infection," Danny said, remembering. "It used to work awfully good when we got cut or something." He turned to Mrs. Beecher and told her the remedy.

She turned and went to the cupboard in the kitchen to begin the preparation.

"Now," Danny said, taking a piece of heavy flannel and soaking it in the solution, "we'll put this on Mr. Beecher's foot. Mom said that it's about as good as anything she's ever seen to take out infection, except penicillin of course."

Mrs. Beecher was looking at the red streak that had started up the sick man's swollen leg – the streak that signaled blood poisoning. Then she felt the hot forehead, and said, "His fever's going up again. Would you get some more snow and melt it, Danny? I'm going to have to bathe him again to get it down."

Danny and Ron opened the door for an instant, shivering in the sudden blast of frigid air, and scooped up a bucket of soft snow, which they put on the stove to melt.

While Mrs. Beecher was busy in the bedroom, Danny, Kay, and the twins knelt beside the stove and began to pray.

"Heavenly Father," Kay prayed first, "You know how sick Mr. Beecher is. And You know how the weather is. We can't get through to get a doctor up here. Just be with him and help him to get through this crisis. May his fever break and–and the infection in his leg go down. And–and Lord Jesus, help us to know what to do to help him…."

Danny prayed next, and then Ron and Roxie. Finally, they were finished and got slowly to their feet.

For several seconds no one spoke. Danny got two or three sticks of wood from the box and built up the fire again, while Kay glanced anxiously toward the bedroom door.

After what seemed to be an hour or more Mrs. Beecher came out. Her face was drawn and haggard.

"How is he?" Kay asked.

"I–I think he's a little better," she answered uncertainly. "It seems to me that his fever has broken. And I don't believe that red streak has gone any further up his leg. And that's a good sign."

"Thank God!" Danny and Kay breathed prayerfully.

None of them slept well that night. The wind raged angrily without a letup and the snow was like a wall of white. The fire had gone down a little during the night, and the windows were covered with frost and ice when Danny turned uncomfortably in his blanket on the floor and looked up.

Mrs. Beecher was already up, changing the pack on her husband's foot.

"He seems to be quite a little better this morning," she whispered as she tiptoed out to the stove to warm the boric acid solution. "And I don't think he has much of a fever."

"That's good," responded Danny.

They had breakfast, sitting close to the little barrel stove to keep warm.

"Do you think we'll be able to get back home today?" Roxie asked nervously. "The folks are going to be terribly worried about us."

"We won't be able to go back to Pine Creek until this storm lets up," Danny told her.

"I was looking out the window a minute ago, and I think it's getting lighter," Ron said. "It doesn't seem to be nearly as thick as it was last night."

Danny Orlis got up and went to the window. Ron was right. The storm had lessened considerably. The wind was still blowing, and the snow was still swirling along the ground in great white billows. But he could see the distinct outline of trees on the other side of Harrison Creek. He could even make out the blurred figure of the air sled, almost submerged by snow.

"Maybe we can make it in a little while," Danny said. "We ought to get home as quickly as we can."

Many of the Angle blizzards lasted for several days, but this one had dumped its load of snow in one wild night and was now blowing itself out. In another hour they could see half a mile up the creek.

"Come on, Ron," Danny said, reaching for his coat and heavy boots. "We'd better start for home."

By the time Danny had pulled on his boots, his younger brother had bundled into his parka.

"You boys had better borrow our snowshoes," Mrs. Beecher said, coming to the bedroom door. "With this soft snow you might not be able to make it on your skis."

They put on the snowshoes and began to trudge through the soft white drifts toward the mouth of Harrison Creek, when they were startled to see a team and a big sled coming toward them in the distance.

"Look!" Ron shouted, pointing at them. "Dad and Mr. Thompson are coming!"

Danny shouted and waved excitedly.

"We're mighty glad to see you guys," Carl Orlis said happily as he and Mr. Thompson came driving up to where the boys were standing.

"We knew you'd be worried," said Danny.

"I told Mom that you'd be at the Beecher cabin, but you know how women are when it comes to worrying," answered his dad.

They went into the cabin and, bundling Mr. Beecher into all the blankets they could find, loaded him into the sled and started for the Orlis home.

By the time they got there, Tex had flown in with the doctor. He examined Mr. Beecher and suggested that they take him outside to the hospital.

"I don't think he's in any danger," he said when

he saw the look of fright on Mrs. Beecher's face. "But he's going to need a lot of patchwork on that leg of his if he's going to be able to use it properly. Then too we should have him where we can watch him."

The doctor and Mr. Beecher were already in the plane and were waiting for Mrs. Beecher when Tex turned to Danny.

"I almost forgot," he said. "I've got a telegram for you."

"A telegram?" the Orlis boy echoed. "Who'd be sending me a telegram?"

"I don't know, but it's from Cedarton."

Hurriedly Danny tore it open. "It's from Coach Collins," he exclaimed. "He wired that he doesn't want me to decide definitely on any college until he gets a chance to talk with me." Danny grinned broadly. "He says he's got an outstanding offer for me."

CHAPTER 7

LOOKING AHEAD TO COLLEGE

The skies cleared over the Angle that afternoon, and early the following morning, Tex flew in to take Danny and Kay back to Cedarton to school.

"How was Mr. Beecher when you got him down to the hospital?" Kay asked the pilot as soon as he got out of the trim little plane.

"He seemed to stand the trip well enough," Tex said, "but that leg of his is in bad shape. I'm afraid that he's going to be in the hospital for a long while."

They got into the plane and Tex took off. The whole Angle country lay in a cloak of dazzling white below them, unbroken except for the gaunt, gray arms of leafless trees, and the little blotches of green that marked the pines and cedars.

"Did I tell you about the telegram I got from Coach Collins yesterday?" Danny asked Kay.

An odd look came over her face.

"Your mom told me about it last night."

"Just think, there are two big schools that want me to come and play football for them. And here I've been worrying about whether I'd have enough money to even think about going on to college next year," Danny continued.

Kay leaned forward and looked out the window of the plane. Then she turned to Danny. "I'd had rather hoped that you would decide to go to a Bible school somewhere."

"But if I go to a Bible school, Kay," Danny protested, "I'd have to pay my own way. And I wouldn't get to play football either. As it is, I can go to an outstanding university, get to play football, and not have any financial worries at all."

"I know that," the girl answered. "But what about good, sound Bible training? That's far more important. In fact, I've heard a lot of outstanding Christian leaders say that it's the most important thing to look for in getting an education if you want to remain true to the Lord."

He eyed her quizzically.

"You sound just like Dad."

"I wish that you'd pray about going to Bible school, Danny," Kay persisted.

"I will," he promised. "But I want to find out what Coach Collins has in mind before I decide anything."

Danny and Kay landed at the Cedarton airport just in time to catch a ride to town and get out to school for the opening of classes. As the Orlis boy came into his homeroom, Tim Barton looked up at him and grinned significantly.

"I've got to see you after class," Tim whispered. "And brother, is it important!"

When the first period was over, Tim joined Danny just outside the classroom door.

"Coach Collins called me into his office this morning," Tim said excitedly. "And guess what! One of the biggest schools in the South wants you and me to come down and play football for them."

Danny fell in beside his friend and they walked to their next class together. "What kind of an offer did they make?" he asked eagerly.

"He didn't say for sure," Tim said, "but he thought that it would be a better deal than what you had been offered at Westbrook."

Danny grinned in spite of himself. "Now that would be something," he replied. "It sounds good to me."

"Me too," Tim answered. "That's the only way I can get to go to college. That's for sure."

During Danny's first study period Coach Collins sent for him.

"Did you get my telegram?" he asked.

The boy nodded.

"You haven't made any definite arrangements about a school for next year, have you?" continued the coach.

"I got another letter from Westbrook," Danny told him. "But I haven't made up my mind definitely."

"That's fine," Mr. Collins replied. "I had a visitor this week from one of the big universities in the South. He made a wonderful offer to you and Tim if you'll go down there to school."

Danny said nothing.

"Did you ever hear of Crestwood U?" The coach leaned forward intently. "They were second in the nation last year. And with the material they've got coming up for the next three or four years they ought to be right at the top of the list. And they're strong enough scholastically to give you a good, sound education."

"Wherever I go to school I'm going to have to have a lot of financial help," Danny said uncertainly. "The way things are I can't depend too much on help from the parents. At least I don't want to."

The coach kept on, "If you take this offer you won't have a financial worry all through college. They'll set you up with a scholarship that will take care of all your books and tuition and spending money. And they'll help you get a job that isn't too difficult. They'll see that you're paid very well for the time that you put in on it. And in addition, there are some wealthy oil men in the alumni association who make a habit of taking care of former football players who have done a good job for them. So there's a chance for you to go into the oil business when you graduate from college, and get a good salary right from the start."

Danny sat there silently. "I didn't think it would be anything like that. I've never heard of such an offer."

The coach leaned back in his chair and smiled broadly. "I know that you can't give an answer on a thing like this today," he said. "But write to your parents and tell them about it. See what they have to say. And then, in a week or two I'll talk with you again."

When Danny left the coach's office his head was whirling. And, during the rest of the day, though he went through the motions of attending class, his mind was far away.

When school was out, he met Tim in the corridor, and the two of them walked home together.

"What do you think of that?" Tim asked. "An offer like that means that I'll be able to go on to college. And all the time I've been figuring that I'd have to go out and get a job just as soon as we graduate."

"Yes, it's tempting, all right," Danny answered. "And what makes it more tempting is the fact that it's one of the best football schools in the country."

"The Lord certainly works things out for us, doesn't He?" Tim said after they had walked a block or so. "I've been praying and praying about getting a job, you know."

Danny nodded.

"Well," continued Tim, "I was talking to Mr. Meyer the other day. I happened to mention that I was going to have to have a job if I wanted to continue going to high school. He suggested that I take over the magazine agency that Mrs. Meyer used to have."

"I don't know why we didn't think of that before,"

Danny told him. "I sold magazines for her last year and did quite well with it."

"I went out just a little while the past couple of days to see how I could do," Tim went on. "And I was really surprised at the number of subscriptions I got."

"That's fine," Danny said. He did not tell Tim that he had been seriously thinking about talking to Mrs. Meyer about taking over the magazine agency himself.

However, that evening Mr. Meyer talked with him.

"I saw Tim the other day. He's taking over the magazine agency so he can earn enough money to stay in school the rest of this term."

"That's what he told me this afternoon," said Danny.

"I've been meaning to talk with you about it," Mr. Meyer continued. "It is a good thing, and I'd hate to see someone else take it up. But I decided that I'd rather have you down at the store with me. One of the clerks quit last week, and instead of hiring another one I thought I'd talk to you about working after school and on Saturday. That is, if you'd like to."

"Boy, would I!"

And then Danny told him about his opportunity to *go* to Crestwood University.

When Mr. Meyer heard about the offer that had been made to the two boys, he was quiet.

"Don't you think it sounds like a good deal?" asked Danny.

"Well," the businessman said slowly, "to tell you the truth, I'm not so sure. If you had asked me this a year ago, I'd have told you to jump at the chance before they change their minds. But things are different now. I'm a Christian. And with Ken having been killed the way he was. I've come to think that there are more important things in life."

Danny looked at him for a long while. Mr. Meyer had something there. But there was one thing he was forgetting. Where would Danny's financial help come from if he did decide to go to Bible school?

* * * *

Back at the Angle several days passed and Mrs. Beecher still hadn't come back to teach school. There had been a letter from her the first of the week, telling them that her husband was going to have to undergo surgery as soon as he was strong enough.

"And," she wrote, "I don't have any idea when I'll be able to leave him and come back to open school again."

"Maybe we aren't going to have any more school this year," Ron said, almost hopefully. "If she doesn't come back, we'll just have to quit for the rest of the year, won't we Dad?"

"If she isn't able to come back until May you can probably go to school all summer," Mr. Orlis teased.

That night before the twins were in bed, Mr. and Mrs. Orlis went out into the kitchen and closed the door.

"This school thing has me concerned, Mary," Carl said. "With an injury like Tom has he could be laid up for a long while. And I don't think that Mrs. Beecher would even consider leaving him in Warroad and coming back here alone."

"But what will we do if she doesn't? We could never get another teacher this time of year." Mrs. Orlis seemed concerned.

Carl Orlis shook his head slowly. "That's the thing that troubles me. I think I'll go back to Warroad tomorrow with Tex and talk to her."

Tex Williams came in the following morning about 10 o'clock, and Ron and Mr. Orlis went down to Warroad with him. Mrs. Beecher was at the hospital when they got there.

"I was just going to write to you," she told Carl Orlis, taking him out into the hall where her husband couldn't hear them. "The doctor tells me that Tom is going to have to undergo a series of two or three very serious operations. He'll be in the hospital for several months."

"That's certainly too bad," said Mr. Orlis.

"I was going to write and tell you that I won't be able to finish the school term," added Mrs. Beecher.

CHAPTER 8

SCHOOL CLOSED AT THE ANGLE

Danny Orlis had promised Coach Collins that he would write to his parents and tell them about the offer to go to Crestwood and play football. He sat down and tried, but somehow, he couldn't put it on paper. It sounded so cold and materialistic only to be thinking of what he could get for playing football, without a thought about learning what God would have him do.

Danny wrote the heading on another clean sheet of paper. He almost knew what his parents would think. They hadn't said much about the offer from Westbrook. On things of that sort, they let him make up his own mind. But there was no mistaking the concern in their faces. All they could think of was a Bible school.

He crumpled the paper before him and threw it into the wastebasket. Why should they care what sort of a school he attended. He was a Christian and had strong ideals when it came to separation. He could go to a school like Crestwood U without hurting his faith. Why didn't they want him to go where he could get a scholarship for playing football, and an easy job that would help him all through school? He got up and strolled to the window. He stood there looking out on the snow-covered street.

He was still standing there when Kirk called him to the telephone.

"I think Kay wants to talk to you."

There was a committee meeting over at Marilyn's which Danny had forgotten all about until that very moment.

"I'll stop by for you in about twenty minutes," he told her. "And we can walk over to Foresters together."

"I don't know why," Kay said as they walked up the steps to the Forester home, "but Marilyn said her dad insisted that we have our committee meeting over here tonight."

"I've got something to show you," Marilyn's dad said proudly, starting toward the basement stairs with them. "Just got it finished tonight."

Danny and Kay looked at him oddly.

"I haven't liked the idea of you kids hanging out at the corner store all the time," he continued. "Not that there's anything wrong with the place, but it doesn't seem good to me for Christian young people to have a hangout up town. So, during Christmas vacation Marilyn and I decided to do something about it."

He opened the door at the foot of the basement stairs and switched on the light.

"Oh!" Kay gasped in astonishment. "It's beautiful!"

Danny Orlis turned slowly about. The room looked very inviting. The walls had been painted, and some sort of inexpensive wallboard had been put in for the other partitions, and an attractive asphalt tile had been laid on the floor. At one end was a large davenport, two or three easy chairs, a radio and MP3 player, and a bookshelf well supplied with Christian books and magazines. At the other end was a ping pong table.

Marilyn came down and joined them. "How do you like it?" she beamed.

"You don't have to have a special invitation to come here," Mr. Forester said. "You can play games or read or hold committee meetings any time. We've got a little stove in the next room for making hot chocolate, and there will always be plenty of ice cream and soft drinks in the refrigerator."

Soon Mr. Forester excused himself and went back upstairs.

Danny sat down in one of the big easy chairs and picked up a current copy of a fine Christian magazine.

"This is really something!" he exclaimed, looking really pleased.

* * * *

The next day, Coach Collins saw Danny in the hall and asked him if he had heard from his parents yet.

"You want to be getting action on this, you know."

"To tell you the truth," Danny admitted, "I haven't written to them yet."

"They're not going to hold that offer open forever," Mr. Collins told him. "They've got a certain number of football scholarships. When those are gone, there won't be any more until the next year. You'd better write your parents today, or you're apt to lose out."

That evening when Danny got off work at the hardware store he went directly to his room and wrote to his mom and dad. He tried to make the offer sound as attractive as possible, but somehow as he went downtown to mail the letter, he felt disturbed and ill at ease.

The following day Coach Collins called him out of the study room again.

"Did you get that letter written to your parents?"

"I wrote last night," Danny replied.

"Fine. I got a letter from Mr. Eckwall. He's the guy who was here to see me about you and Tim. He's going to be in Minneapolis next week. And if you're really interested in going down there, he'll come up and talk with you personally."

"I–I'll have to let you know," was all the boy could say.

When Danny finally got home from school that day there was a letter from home waiting for him. It gave him a little start at first, until he remembered that it couldn't be an answer to the letter he had written only the day before.

"And so," his mom wrote, "Dad checked with the University and the Teacher's College in St. Cloud and wasn't able to find a single teacher who would come up here. There was only one who was interested, and she refused to come when she found out where the Northwest Angle is.

"This problem of a school for Ron and Roxie for the rest of the year is serious, Danny. Won't you pray with us that things will work out in accord with God's will?"

There was more to the letter, but Danny didn't read the rest of it at the moment. He sat there, staring at his mom's neat handwriting.

"What's the matter, Danny?" Mr. Meyer asked, coming in from the kitchen. "Is there something wrong at home?"

Danny shook his head. "No. I mean there isn't any sickness or anything like that. It's just that the school up home has had to close, and there isn't any place for the twins to go." He told Mr. Meyer what had happened to the teacher's husband, and how she had been forced to leave at mid-term.

"What grade are the twins in?"

"They're in the eighth grade, so this is their last year up there. That's one thing that makes it so bad."

Mr. Meyer smiled thoughtfully. "I wouldn't worry too much about it if I were you," he said. "Things like that have a way of working out if we just keep our trust in the Lord."

They had had the young people's meeting over at Marilyn's, and Danny and Kay and several of the others were sitting around talking, when Kay asked, "Are any of you going out to see the new Cedarton Bible Institute?"

Danny looked at her.

"I'd heard something about the new school, but I didn't know it was ready to start yet, or that they even had anything out there to look at."

"They bought the old children's home building," Kay said, "and are completely remodeling it. I think they're moving the school here from some place in the southern part of the state."

"It would be fun to go out and see what it's all about," Marilyn said. "I don't know whether I'd be interested in it or not, but I'd certainly like to see what they have to offer."

"Danny and I have another school that we're interested in," Tim said. "Haven't we, Danny?"

"You don't need to be so secretive about it," Rick Haines said. "We know all about it. You aren't fooling us. You're going down south and playing football."

"Sounds like a pretty good deal to me too," Tim answered, smiling. "Beats selling magazines."

Kay's gaze met Danny's. He looked away quickly.

They decided that they would go out to the Bible school one evening that week, but first one thing and then another came up to interfere. Tim had been doing very well selling magazines and he had some appointments. Danny had an English theme to make up, and Mr. Meyer decided that he wanted the displays in the store windows changed. That took two evenings. So they weren't able to make it.

Danny didn't particularly care. In fact, he was glad that they hadn't been able to go out and visit the Bible school. He was uncomfortable every time he thought of it.

But he made the matter of a school for Ron and Roxie a definite subject of prayer. Every morning and evening he knelt and prayed. He didn't realize that his concern was so apparent, but Mr. Meyer noticed it.

"You are worried about a school for your brother and sister, aren't you, Danny?"

"It's so expensive to go to a private school," the boy said, "that I know my parents won't be able to send them."

Mr. Meyer leaned back and crossed his legs.

"How do you think they'd like to go to school here in Cedarton?" he asked. "Mrs. Meyer and I talked it over this evening. If you'll help take the responsibility for the twins, to see that they don't do things your parents won't approve of, we'd be very happy to have them come and live with us."

CHAPTER 9

FOOTBALL OR BIBLE?

Danny Orlis went upstairs and wrote to his parents that evening. "We just couldn't find a better place. And the twins would be in a real Christian home."

Danny watched the mailbox anxiously. And before the end of the week he got a letter from his mom saying that she and the twins would be flying down to Cedarton Saturday morning. "This is a real answer to prayer, Danny," she wrote.

She mentioned the Crestwood offer too. He pursed his lips as he read that. Just as he had thought, she and Dad wouldn't tell him what to do.

"I think you know what we both think about it, Danny," the letter read, "but the decision is yours. We want you to do what you feel is best, according to God's will for your life."

* * * *

Mrs. Meyer worked hard to get things ready for the twins. "Ron can share Kirk's room," she told Danny Friday evening, "and Roxie can room with Karen."

The next morning when Tex flew in with the twins and his mom, Danny and Mrs. Meyer were waiting at the airport.

"Boy!" Ron exclaimed excitedly, crawling out of the plane and running across the frozen snow to Danny. "It's going to be swell going to school here with you. Do they have any basketball teams for guys my age?"

"Sure thing," Danny said, ruffling his brother's hair.

Roxie smiled shyly as she took his hand.

"Are you glad that you're going to go to school here in Cedarton?" he asked her.

For an instant she was silent. "I–I think so."

"You can't be getting homesick already," her twin said, scoffing. "We're going to be here for months and months and months."

Roxie looked up at Danny. "I guess if you and Kay are here, I won't get so homesick."

On Monday morning Danny took the twins to school and helped them get registered for classes.

"I can take them," Kirk volunteered. "I know my way around up there at school."

"I think Danny had better take them this first morning, Kirk," Mrs. Orlis told him. "There are some things I want him to tell Mr. Brown about the subjects they have been taking."

That afternoon after school Danny was a little late

getting down to the lower hall where Ron and Roxie were to wait for him. He thought they might have gone on home with Kirk and Karen, but they were still standing at the side door, looking up the corridor nervously.

"I thought you'd gone and left us, Danny," Ron said. "We were just about ready to start home."

"Maybe Ron was," Roxie said firmly, "but I wasn't, unless you, or Kirk, or Karen, or somebody came to walk with us."

"You used to find your way around Iron Mountain," laughed Danny.

"But that was different," insisted the girl.

"You'll get onto Cedarton in a couple of days, Roxie," Danny said. "Anybody who can get around the Angle the way you do doesn't have to worry about a little town like this."

It was two or three days later when Danny came home and Ron met him at the door.

"Coach Collins has been calling for you. He says for you to call him right away. It's important."

Danny went to the telephone. He knew what the coach wanted. And he didn't have an answer for him.

"But, Danny," the coach said almost angrily, "you've got to make up your mind. We can't hold off Crestwood much longer. If you've got a better offer let me know. I might be able to get Crestwood to do just a little better."

"It isn't that."

"Then what is it?"

"I—I just don't know whether I want to go to that kind of a school or not," he answered lamely.

"Well," the coach retorted, "Mr. Eckwall is going to be here soon. And when he comes, he's going to expect an answer."

Danny stood in the living room for a moment after talking on the phone. Then he turned and went slowly upstairs.

"Is everything all right?" Ron asked him.

Danny grinned crookedly and ran his fingers through the boy's hair.

"Yes," he said, "everything's all right. It's just that I've got to make a decision on a certain thing before long. And I don't know what to do."

"If it's about that football deal," Ron said quickly, "I know what you ought to do. Grab that scholarship quick before they change their minds."

In his room that evening Danny knelt beside the bed and tried to pray the matter through. But somehow he couldn't get any satisfaction. And when he got to his feet he was still as disturbed as ever.

The next evening was Young People's. Danny and Kay walked home together, as usual.

"… and so," he concluded, telling her about the phone call from Coach Collins, "it looks as though Tim and I are going to have to decide about this school business one way or another. And right away." They walked slowly through the snow. For a time, neither of them spoke.

"I guess I'll feel better once I make up my mind," Danny went on. "Then I can begin to think about something else."

"Have you given up the idea of attending the Bible Institute here at Cedarton?" Kay asked hesitantly. "It's a very good school, Danny. You ought to look into it before you definitely decide on anything."

"I've considered a Bible Institute," the boy told her, "but I've decided to spend my time working on a degree. I hate to waste time in a Bible Institute."

"You won't be wasting your time, Danny," came Kay's answer. "It's never a waste of time to study the Word of God."

"But it takes so long to get a degree, Kay," he said, "that I hate to spend time in school that won't count toward it."

"Why don't you go out with us tomorrow night and see what they've got to offer?"

Tim and Danny had almost decided that they couldn't go out to the Bible Institute with the rest of the gang. But when Rick and Eddie Masters came for them, they put their studies aside and went along.

Danny was very much surprised with the facilities at the Cedarton Bible Institute. They had large, well-lit classrooms, a good library, and a well-equipped gymnasium. But it was a little room on the third floor that fascinated Danny.

"This is our prayer room," the school president, who was showing them around, explained.

The catalog Danny had seen from Crestwood U told a great deal about the sororities and fraternities, the big dances they held, and the good times the students had. Somehow the contrast startled him.

"You know, Dr. Anders," Tim said, "there's one thing that bothers me a great deal about Bible institutes. I don't like the idea of spending a year or two here and not being able to transfer my credits to another school to get my degree."

"But you can transfer a great many of them," Dr. Anders told him. "And we're raising our standards all the time."

Tim turned to Danny. "That does make a difference, doesn't it?"

Danny did not answer him.

That night after the Orlis boy got home, he was more disturbed than ever. He had almost made himself believe that he had to go to Crestwood U. But after seeing the Bible Institute he wasn't so sure. He tossed restlessly on the bed for an hour or so before drifting off to sleep.

By the end of the week Ron and Roxie were getting on so well that Mrs. Orlis decided to go back to the Angle.

She held Roxie close to her for a long minute and gave Ron a kiss on the tip of his nose.

Roxie cried a little as they went back to the Meyers' home after Tex took off with Mrs. Orlis. But by the time they stepped into the big, friendly house again, she had wiped away the tears and was smiling bravely.

Coach Collins talked with Danny and Tim two or three times about going to Crestwood during the next few days.

"It's just like I told you," he explained. "They've got a limited number of football scholarships. They're going to use them to get the best talent available. So if you want to go to school down there, you're going to have to make up your minds."

"When did you say that scout was coming?" Danny asked.

"I had another phone call from him. He had to postpone his trip to Minneapolis for a little while, but he thinks now that he'll be here in a week or ten days." The coach got up and came around to the other side of the desk.

"For the life of me I can't figure out what's the matter with you guys. Here you are with an offer from one of the best football schools in the country and you can't make up your minds whether you want to go or not. Anyone else on the team would jump at the chance."

On Friday evening it seemed that everybody in town went to the basketball game. Danny and Kay, Marilyn and Eddie Masters, and Tim and a new girl who had just moved into town a few weeks before, all went to the game together. And the rest of the gang joined them for a victory party in the Forester basement.

"Oh, that was a wonderful game, Rick!" Kay said as the tall, lanky basketball star came in.

"I believe it was the best game I ever saw you play," Marilyn added.

Rick grinned self-consciously. "I just got hot."

Danny complimented him too and went over to a chair in the corner and sat down. It wasn't that he was jealous of Rick. But it did set him to thinking.

That was the way it would be if they went to Crestwood to school, only nationally known newspapers would be writing about them. And if Crestwood had a good team for the next three or four years, and if he didn't get hurt, he just might be fortunate enough to make one of the All-American teams.

It was a real temptation.

Later that evening, when he and Kay were walking home he told her what he had decided.

"Are–are you sure that's what you want to do?" she asked. "Have you definitely made up your mind?"

"I'm going to Crestwood," Danny said simply.

Kay was silent the rest of the way home.

The next day was Saturday. She went over to the parsonage, as soon as she had helped with the work at the house where she stayed, to talk with the new pastor and his wife.

"And Danny and Tim are both going to Crestwood U so they can play football," Kay finished.

Pastor Arnold turned toward the window and looked out across the snow-covered street. "I'm terribly disappointed. I've been hoping both boys would go on to Bible school before going to college."

"That's what we've been talking to them about," Kay said, "but it doesn't seem to do any good."

The pastor took a deep breath.

"But what are we going to do?" Kay asked, bewildered.

"There is only one thing we can do," he told her.

"And that's to take it to the Lord in prayer."

Together Kay, the pastor, and his wife knelt in the living room.

CHAPTER 10

SEEDS OF DOUBT

Danny Orlis thought that deciding on a school would ease his mind, that he would be able to turn his attention to other things – his responsibilities at the store, at Young People's, and his studies. But over the weekend he was just as disturbed as ever. Every time he knelt to pray, or sat down to read his Bible, it seemed as though an invisible barrier had been thrown up between him and the Lord.

Monday afternoon when he got home from school, he saw a note on his desk that Ron had left for him.

"Important! Call Pastor Arnold at his home right away. Important!"

When he got the minister on the phone it didn't seem as important as Ron had made it sound. Mr. Arnold wanted Danny and Tim to go and call on Bill Martin, a young man who had come to church and Sunday school a year or so ago but hadn't been there for several months.

"I thought that a couple of you guys might be able to make him see that we need him," the minister said. "I don't really know whether Bill is a Christian or not. He never did make a public profession from all I've been able to learn. And the day I was over there he avoided the subject. But I've been told that at one time he was very much interested in the Word of God."

"We'll be glad to go," Danny agreed. "I'll find Tim, and we'll see Bill this evening."

"I knew I could count on you," the pastor replied.

Danny and Tim had planned to get together that evening to study. He called Tim and they met on a street corner and went across town to the place where Bill Martin lived with his parents.

"I don't think I've ever seen Bill around the church," Tim said, as they approached the big brick house at the end of the street. "Has he been around any since I've been going there?"

"I don't think so," said Danny. "As I understand it, he used to attend quite regularly. But I only recall seeing him in church at Christmas and Easter since I've been in Cedarton. He's been away for the past two or three years going to school or something."

Bill's mom invited the boys into the living room and called her son. In a moment or two he came down. He was a tall, handsome young man, a couple of years or so older than they were, with broad shoulders and a ready smile.

"Hi, fellas!" he said easily. "What can I do for you?"

Danny cleared his throat.

"Pastor Arnold asked us to come over and visit you," he said. "He said that he's been told you used to attend Sunday school with us several years ago. We'd like to give you a special invitation to come back."

Bill Martin leaned back in his chair and crossed his legs.

"We've got some fine Sunday school classes," Tim put in. "I know you'd like it. And Pastor Arnold has been bringing some wonderful messages lately. We– we need guys like you."

"I used to go to church over there," Bill explained. "Went to Young People's, Sunday school, church – the whole works."

"We'd certainly like to have you come back again," Danny told him.

Bill Martin was silent for a time.

"Come to think of it," he said, finally, "I sort of miss going over there. There was a time when I would have gone down to the altar and have taken Christ as my Savior if someone would have asked me. In fact, several of my best friends did go forward." He paused, and a faraway look came into his eyes. "I'm glad now that I didn't. I got down to the U full of silly ideas about the Bible and this Christian business, but they soon set me straight."

"W-w-what do you mean?" Danny asked.

"I must have believed about the way you guys do," Bill continued. There was a strange wistfulness in his voice, as though he envied Danny and Tim their faith. "I had always been taught that the Bible was the Word of God, and absolutely true, the one Book that was unchangeable. But when I got into some of my classes I found out how far behind the times I really was. I learned that the Bible is only a collection of myths and misstatements and half-truths. It's a wonderful piece of literature, but that's all."

For almost a minute the three of them sat in the quiet living room, staring at one another awkwardly.

Bill Martin leaned forward.

"Christ is a wonderful Teacher, and a great Example for all of us," he went on. "Probably the best Example this world has ever had. But this being the Son of God is another thing." He shook his head. "I found out at the U that everything I had been believing was a bunch of foolishness. That's when I quit going to Sunday school and church."

Bill Martin had more to say about the Bible and the Lord Jesus Christ. He talked almost longingly about the days when he had believed the Bible and had been so very close to making a decision for Christ.

"But there's no use kidding myself," he concluded as they arose to go. "I just couldn't believe the Bible now. Not after what I've been taught."

When Danny and Tim were finally outside their heads were reeling.

"Did you hear what he said?" Tim asked. "It almost makes me afraid to even think about going to Crestwood."

"But that sort of thing wouldn't happen to you and me," Danny said bravely. "We've been taught better than that. We know that the Bible is the Word of God, and that Christ is the Son of God. It wouldn't make any difference if we did get into a class or two where they taught counter to the Bible. I know it wouldn't shake my faith."

There was a long silence.

"I don't think I would be swayed by things like that either," agreed Tim.

Every time Danny closed his eyes that night he could see the haunted look on Bill Martin's face, as he talked so wistfully about the days when he had believed that the Bible was the Word of God. Of course, Bill hadn't been a Christian. That would make a big difference. It was different with him. And yet it could ruin his testimony.

Finally, Danny Orlis drifted off to sleep. But when he awakened in the morning he still felt as if a lump of lead were lying in the pit of his stomach. He got up wearily and went down to breakfast.

That same feeling of uneasiness stayed with him as he went to school and hung his coat in the locker. His faith was the most important thing in the world to him. What would happen if he went to Crestwood without being thoroughly grounded in the Word of God?

That morning during the first period Coach Collins sent for him and Tim.

"Well," he began, "I got a telephone call from a Mr. Davis last night. He's the Crestwood representative who finally made the trip up into this area instead of Mr. Eckwall."

The boys nodded.

"He wants to meet with you before you reach a definite decision," Mr. Collins went on. "I thought he had made you as good an offer as anybody could hope for, but he said that they are so short of back-field material that he's willing to go all out to get you two to go to Crestwood."

"Well," Tim said uncertainly, "I think I know what I'm going to do, but it probably won't hurt us to listen to what he has to say."

Danny nodded in agreement.

"That's fine," the coach said, beaming. "Neither of you will ever regret choosing Crestwood. It's the finest football school you'll find anywhere. Look at a list of the All-American teams down through the years and notice how many of the guys played for them. No other school in the country has a better record."

Danny began to warm up a little. Crestwood was willing to make them a better offer than they had before. He might even be able to lay up a little money while he went there to school.

The coach looked at his watch.

"I've got to run. I'm supposed to meet Mr. Davis down at the hotel. Why don't you guys come down there about 6:30 this evening? We'll all go out to the Steak House for dinner. Then you can talk with Mr. Davis yourselves and see what kind of an offer he has for you."

Danny was so excited at the thought of going to Crestwood and playing on a big-time football team that he forgot all about Bill Martin. In fact, he practically forgot about his studies too, and dreamed his way through a history test. He only got a *D* when the rest of his work in the class had been *A* and *B*.

Tim sat across the aisle from Danny Orlis, and the moment the dismissal bell rang he was on his feet.

"I've got to go home and change my clothes," he said. "And I want to tell Mom about meeting Mr. Davis. Boy, this is going to be swell! Getting to go to school and not having to worry about money."

"And who'd ever think that we'd get paid for playing football?" Danny added. "Especially with a school like Crestwood."

* * * *

Mr. Davis was a big, pleasant chap with a hearty laugh and a smile for everybody.

"Your coach tells me that you guys are seriously considering Crestwood U," he said, as they sat down at the table. "Well, you won't be making a mistake. I can tell you that much."

The waitress came in with the menus, but Mr. Davis waved them aside.

"Just bring us four of the biggest T-bone steaks you've got in the house," he ordered. "And give us plenty of French fries on the side."

The waitress took Mr. Davis at his word. She brought out four of the largest steaks either of the boys had ever seen.

"Fill up, fellas," urged Mr. Davis. "While you eat, think about the training table down at Crestwood. This is the way we feed our boys. Nothing is too good for them."

Tim looked at Danny and grinned. When they had finished eating, Mr. Davis got around to talking terms.

"I've been saving this as a little surprise," he said, "but your coach tells me that you've been thinking of going somewhere else. So I thought that I'd better tell you about the rest of our offer." He stopped and took a deep breath. "We've got an automobile dealer in our town who thinks an awful lot of our football players. In fact, he thinks so much of them that he's told me he will present new convertibles to a very few of our top-grade freshmen."

"A–a car?" Danny echoed in disbelief. "You mean that you'd give us a car, on top of everything else you've offered us?"

Mr. Davis nodded. "It doesn't sound possible, does it? But we take care of our boys. And in addition, we've got a filling station owner who sees to it that our guys get a liberal discount on gasoline, oil, tires, and things of that sort. He's been known to tear up the bills of a guy who's out there giving Crestwood U everything he's got."

"And," Coach Collins put in, "this is all on the level. I wouldn't have brought Mr. Davis around if it hadn't been."

For a long minute neither of the boys could speak.

"That sounds a little better than Cedarton Bible Institute, doesn't it, Danny?" Tim asked.

"You guys weren't actually thinking of going to a Bible school, were you?" Mr. Davis asked, laughing. "That isn't what I've been bidding against, is it?"

Danny felt the color rush to his cheeks.

Mr. Davis and the coach laughed heartily.

"You know," the Crestwood representative said, "I used to go to a fanatical church when I was a kid. They preached that the Bible was true and all that sort of thing. Believe it or not I almost got 'saved,' or whatever they call it. At least I was mighty close. I believed that Christ was God's Son, and that He died for sin, and all that sort of thing."

Coach Collins grinned broadly.

"What happened, Don?" he asked. "I never knew you to have a lot of religion."

For an instant, the smile fled from the university representative's face. "To tell you the truth, I went down to Crestwood. And I soon got that stuff knocked out of me."

Danny Orlis straightened quickly, staring across the table at Tim. His face went pale.

CHAPTER 11

A FIRM STAND

There was a strained, unnatural silence at the little table. Coach Collins looked quickly from Mr. Davis to the boys, and back again.

"But you still have a measure of faith, don't you, Don?" the coach asked. "You still go to church and things like that, don't you?"

"Oh, sure!" Mr. Davis answered, catching the concern in the coach's voice. "The only thing is that I'm not so–so… well shall we say that I'm not so fanatical anymore."

"What about your trust in the Bible, Mr. Davis?" Danny Orlis asked. "What did Crestwood do to that?"

Mr. Davis coughed nervously and managed an odd little laugh.

"It didn't ruin my faith, if that's what you're driving at," he said uneasily. "I still consider myself a Christian man. I believe that the Bible contains the Word of

God, and that much of it is true. Let's say that college gave me an enlightened approach to the Bible and the Christian philosophy. It knocked out the superstition and unscientific ideas, and gave me a good, solid, reasonable faith. It's that fanatical stuff like believing that there's a real Hell, and that everyone is a sinner and needs a Savior that I quit believing."

Danny Orlis looked over at Tim as the Crestwood representative began to rummage in his briefcase. He found two applications and handed them to the boys.

"Don't give a second thought to this religion business," Mr. Davis assured them. "It isn't going to hurt your faith to go to the university. In fact, it'll strengthen it."

"The way yours was strengthened?" Danny blurted out before he realized how rude the question must have sounded.

The color drained from Mr. Davis' cheeks, and for a moment or two he could not speak.

"You can fill out these applications tonight," he said lamely. "I'll stop at the school and pick them up in the morning."

Danny Orlis glanced at the long, printed form for a moment, then handed it back to the school official.

"I'm sorry, Mr. Davis," he said evenly, "but I won't be needing this. I'm not going to enroll at Crestwood."

"You're not letting what I said about religion upset you, are you?" Mr. Davis asked him. "I didn't mean it the way it must have sounded. Why, I consider

Crestwood a Christian school. Even though we don't have any church affiliation, as a school we very definitely recognize the value of religion. We've got two or three courses in Bible that are taught right on the campus, and many of our instructors are religious people."

"I'm afraid that Crestwood doesn't offer the sort of Bible training that I want, Mr. Davis," the Orlis boy answered. "I've just come to see how important it is for me to get a thorough grounding in the Word of God before I even think about any other school."

Coach Collins, who had been sitting silently during the discussion, leaned forward. "Is that final?"

Danny nodded.

"How about you, Tim? Are you going to hand that new convertible and a free college education back to me?" the Crestwood representative asked. "That's what that application is, Tim. A brand-new convertible!"

Tim Barton looked at Danny wistfully.

"I had made up my mind that I wasn't going to Crestwood unless Danny did," he said uncertainly.

"But you can't let Danny Orlis ruin everything for you," Coach Collins exclaimed, laying his arm across the back of his star quarterback's chair. "This is your chance to make good, fella. Going to Crestwood can set you up for life."

Tim turned the application over in his hand. "I don't know what to do," he replied. "I want to go to school with Danny. But I–I might not get to go to college at all unless I get this offer."

"You've got to think things out for yourself," the coach continued. "Just because Danny is bent on throwing his life away, there's no reason why you should. You've got more sense than that."

Tim pushed back from the table and folded the application form carefully. "I'll have to think it over."

"That's a good idea," Mr. Davis told him. "That's a mighty fine idea. You think about it and talk it over with your mom. She'll give you good advice."

The senior quarterback looked up quickly.

"She doesn't care what I do."

The two men pushed back from the table.

"I'll drive out to see you tomorrow morning before I leave town, Tim," Mr. Davis said, picking up the check. "And you'd better decide to take me up on this proposition and go down to Crestwood to school.

They really need you, and from what Mr. Collins has told me you need Crestwood."

Tim did not answer him.

"And if you change your mind, Danny, see Mr. Collins first thing in the morning. He can get in touch with me," added Mr. Davis quickly.

"I won't be changing my mind," the Orlis boy said firmly.

Mr. Davis paid the check. The two boys put on their coats and walked out into the chilly night air.

"What was the big idea, Danny?" Tim wanted to

know when they were alone. "We talked it over. And we both decided that we were going to Crestwood. What's the matter with you?"

"I just couldn't do it, Tim," explained Danny. "I tried to kid myself into thinking that it would be all right for me to go down there to school. I tried to tell myself that it wouldn't hurt my testimony. That I was too strong to be weakened. Now I know that I've got to go to a school where I'll get good, solid grounding in the Word of God – a school where I'll be able to study the Bible under consecrated, Bible believing teachers."

"But it won't hurt your faith to go to Crestwood," Tim countered. "You heard what Mr. Davis said."

"Look what happened to his faith," argued Danny. "I guess I shouldn't say that, because I don't think that he had any real faith in the first place. But at least he's gotten to the point now where I doubt that the Gospel will ever be able to reach him."

Tim stopped and faced Danny, his eyes blazing.

"You're just like he said," he snapped. "You're a fanatic, Danny Orlis. That's what's wrong with you."

"We don't want to quarrel, Tim," Danny said. "That isn't going to get us any place."

Tim turned on his heel and walked up the street alone. For an instant or two his young friend stared after him. Then Danny crossed the snow-packed street and went up the block to the Meyer home.

* * * *

Danny had intended to stop by Tim's house on the way to school the following morning and talk with him again about Crestwood. But he got up a little late and was still eating breakfast when Tim knocked on the front door and asked for him.

Danny got his coat, and the two of them went down the stairs together. Once or twice the Orlis boy started to say something, but the odd, strained look in Tim Barton's eyes stopped him.

Finally, after they had crossed the street and walked single file through the snow that was still on the sidewalk in front of a vacant lot, Tim said. "Have you thought any more about going to Crestwood?"

Danny nodded.

"To tell you the truth I could hardly get to sleep last night," he admitted.

"Just think how much fun we'd have if we were both down there together, Danny," Tim said eagerly. "Why don't you change your mind? Why don't you sign that application and go down there with me?"

The Orlis boy shook his head.

"I know that we'd have a lot of fun," he agreed. "And I want to play college football more than just about anything else. But I can't bring myself to go to a school like that. I want my faith to be strengthened, not weakened."

"But going to Crestwood isn't going to hurt our

faith," Tim retorted hotly. "You heard what Mr. Davis said. And besides, how are we going to withstand the temptations that come to all of us if we can't withstand the temptations of a school like Crestwood?"

"We've gone all over this before," came Danny's quiet answer. "And as far as I'm concerned it always comes out the same. I shouldn't even have given a serious thought to going to any other sort of school until after I've had a good, solid grounding in the Word of God."

"I was just thinking," Tim went on eagerly. "We wouldn't have to join a fraternity if we didn't want to. It would be a lot of fun, and I don't see what harm it would do. But if you thought it would be better for us, we could leave the frats alone. We could get a room in a private home where you and I were the only university fellows. We wouldn't have all those temptations that way."

But Danny shook his head again.

"I'm sorry, Tim," he replied, "but it's all settled. I'm going to school here in Cedarton."

His companion was crestfallen.

"I'd like to see you think seriously about going to school here too," Danny continued. "You need a lot of training in the Scriptures, so you'll be able to talk with your parents about the Lord Jesus."

"Well," Tim snapped, "you can go to Cedarton Bible Institute for all I care. I'm going to make something of myself. I'm going to Crestwood where I can play football."

With that Tim left Danny and hurried up a side street toward the schoolhouse. Danny watched him go. A lump rose in his throat, and he swallowed hard.

He saw Tim several times in school that day, but his friend refused to speak to him.

That evening after school Danny waited for Kay in the corridor.

"Hello, stranger," she said, smiling as she came up to him. "It's been a long time since I've seen you."

"I've had a lot of things on my mind lately," came Danny's answer, as he fell into step beside her.

"Did you get them settled?" Kay asked, knowingly.

"Yes," Danny told her. "I had a hard time doing it, but I finally got it all settled. I've given up going to school in Crestwood."

"You have?"

"I've finally decided to do what I should have decided right from the first. I'm going to the Bible Institute."

A smile broke across Kay's face. "Oh, that's wonderful!"

"I don't know why I made such a problem of it," Danny continued. "I can see now that it shouldn't have been a difficult choice at all. It's much more important to be in the Lord's will than to go to a school where I can play football."

Tim Barton rode by with several guys just then. Danny and Kay both waved at him. He looked their way, but acted as though he hadn't even seen them.

"Now what's the matter with him? I've never seen him act that way before," Kay wondered.

"He's just mad because I'm not going to Crestwood to school with him," explained the young man.

"He isn't going there alone, is he?" she gasped. "He's just a new Christian. It will be so hard for him to keep them from swamping him with all the temptations and liberal arguments about the Bible."

"I know that it would be hard enough for me," Danny answered. "So hard that I wouldn't want to risk it. But I can't talk to him about it anymore. He only gets mad."

That night at the Forester home, Danny and Kay and the others, who were planning to attend Cedarton Bible Institute in the fall, decided to go out to the school again the following weekend to make application for entrance.

"I'm sure that our grades are all right," Danny said, "and we'll get the recommendations we need. But we ought to get our applications in so that they'll hold space for us."

* * * *

The story that Tim Barton had accepted a scholarship to attend Crestwood spread like a prairie fire throughout the school.

"You mean that they're going to give you free tuition and spending money?" one of the guys was saying admiringly to Tim, as Danny walked past them in the hall. "And all you've got to do is play football for them? You don't mean it? You're kidding us."

"If you think I'm kidding, just ask Coach Collins," Tim said, drawing himself up proudly. "He's the one who lined it up for me. Wrote down to Crestwood and told them all about me. They sent a guy up here the first thing, just to talk to me."

Danny stopped at his locker to get his things.

"And," Tim continued, "getting free tuition and board and room and spending money isn't all. I'm going to get a brand-new convertible too. All my own."

"Whoa!" his companion gasped.

"And that's not all," Tim kept on as the crowd around him grew. "There's a guy down there who sees that the football players get tires, gas and accessories at cost. I'll tell you, they really take care of their players."

"And you say that Orlis turned it down? What's the matter with him anyway?" asked another.

"He's afraid a school like that will hurt his precious faith," Tim retorted, loudly enough so Danny, who was almost to the outside door by this time, could hear.

"I could stand to have my faith hurt a little for a deal like that. How about you, Tim?" shouted still another.

"You didn't see that stopping me, did you?" he demanded.

Danny's ears were burning.

So that was what the guys thought? Perhaps—?

For a brief instant fear that he had made an unwise choice gripped Danny. Roughly he forced it out of his mind. If only he could get Tim to go to the Bible Institute too.

CHAPTER 12

VICTORY OVER SELF

Tim Barton's fame around Cedarton high school mushroomed in the days that followed, as word that he was going to Crestwood on a football scholarship spread. He had always been popular enough at school. But now that he was going to play football for a great university, and on a scholarship at that, his reputation grew rapidly.

Businessmen who seldom recognized him on the street stopped to talk to him. Now and then one of them picked him up on the way to school. He was a guest at the noon meeting of the Men's Business Club and was called into the office of the county attorney who tried to talk him into going to a college out West.

"I called my former coach at Ralston," the attorney said. "I told him what a terrific football player you are, Tim."

The young quarterback smiled proudly.

"He told me that they have a place for you. You can go to school on the west coast under a setup that will beat anything Crestwood has offered you," continued the man.

"I wish I'd known about this before I told Mr. Davis that I'd go to Crestwood to school," Tim said regretfully. "But I've given my word, and I don't want to back out on it."

"Perhaps you don't have anything to back out of," the attorney persisted.

"I signed an application blank, if that's what you mean," Tim told him, "and some sort of paper about the scholarship. I don't know just what it was. Of course, nothing about the car, or the job, or that sort of thing was mentioned in the papers. It's sort of under the table."

The attorney got to his feet.

"If you feel obligated to Crestwood, that's one thing. But if you don't, you aren't under any legal obligation to them. I'd certainly like to have a representative from Ralston talk with you before you decide definitely. It will be worth your while."

"I've already decided definitely. I'm sorry," said Tim, somewhat reluctantly.

The boy's head was swimming as he left the office. To think he was the one the attorney was talking about. He was the one who was being offered still another scholarship, and a job, and he didn't know what all, just to play football. His head was still in the clouds when Danny met him on the street.

"Hi, Tim!" Danny said, almost hesitantly.

Tim Barton drew himself up and turned disdainfully away.

"Why did Danny Orlis have to be so high and mighty?" Tim asked himself, his temper rising. "It wouldn't hurt either of us to go to Crestwood to school. We could play football together, and maybe make All-American together. But no, Danny had to show everyone what a wonderful, sacrificing Christian he was. He had to show everybody what a fanatic he could be!"

Tim crossed the street and entered the corner store. "I don't know why I ever wanted that dope for a friend in the first place," he stormed.

At home some two or three evenings later, Mr. Meyer picked up the Minneapolis paper and turned to the sports page.

"Did you see this item about Tim, Danny?" he asked.

The young man shook his head. He hadn't read the item, but all he had heard during the past two or three weeks had been about Tim Barton. How wonderful it was that poor Tim got such a break that he could go on to school! What a wonderful football player he must be to get the sort of offer Crestwood U had made!

"It says here that at least half a dozen schools have called in their scouts and 'scrubbed' them out good for not getting to Cedarton to take a look at speedster Tim Barton before Crestwood sewed him up," Mr. Meyer read.

"Some of the guys have been talking about that at school," Danny told him. It was bad enough hearing about Tim everywhere he went, let alone at home. He went upstairs.

Tim was absent from Young People's the next time they met. Kay asked Danny about him on the way home.

"I wish there was something we could do to get him interested again," she said. "He's such a new Christian that I'm afraid he'll drift a long way from the way he ought to live, if he doesn't stay under the influence of the church."

"There isn't anything I can do about him," Danny answered curtly. "There's no use asking me. I don't know what's the matter with him."

Kay turned quickly and looked at Danny. It wasn't so much what he had said, but rather the bitterness in his voice that astonished her.

"Why, Danny!" she exclaimed. "I've never heard you use that tone of voice when you talked about anyone!"

"I can't help it!" he retorted, his temper rising. "I've been talked about and lied about and ridiculed over this football deal until I've had about all that I can stand. Do you know what Tim's been telling about me? The guys say that he's telling everyone that the only reason Crestwood offered me a contract was so they could get him. They didn't want me to play for them at all." Danny took a deep breath. "I'm not going to take much more of it," he snapped.

Kay looked at him gravely.

They stopped at the corner store for a dish of ice cream on their way home. Some of the guys called Danny over to their booth.

"Hi, Orlis!" Dick Bridges called. "How does it come that you're not going to Crestwood with Tim?"

"I'd rather go to another school," Danny said uncomfortably.

"Is it true that they didn't really give you an offer at all? That they were using you to get Tim?" continued Dick in a sarcastic tone.

"They offered me a scholarship all right," Danny said, flushing hotly. "But I turned it down to go to Cedarton Bible Institute."

"That's a laugh," shouted Dick.

"It happens to be true," Danny shouted back.

"That's not what Tim says."

"I don't care what Tim says," Danny snapped. "I got another offer from Westbrook too. And they weren't even interested in Tim. At least they didn't contact him. And they scouted us three times."

The smile left Dick's face, and his mouth narrowed to a thin, hard line.

"You really think that you're all right, don't you, preacher boy?" he went on, sneering. "If you've got such fine, beautiful, brotherly love, how does it come that you and your Christian friend Tim aren't loving each other so much anymore?"

The color drained from Danny's cheeks.

"That's a personal matter," he managed lamely.

"Sure," Dick went on, speaking loud enough so that everyone in that end of the store could hear, "you guys preach good. You're always talking about how much the Lord means to you, and how you let Him rule your lives and a lot of baloney like that. But when it comes right down to it, you're not any different than the rest of us."

Danny clenched his fists. Kay laid her hand on his arm.

"Come on, Danny," she whispered.

"Sure," Dick continued. "Take him away now, Kay. Take him away so he doesn't let that precious Christian temper get the best of him."

Danny's shoulders were trembling, and the perspiration was standing out on his forehead. His mouth was hot and dry.

"Come on, Kay. Let's get out of here," he stammered.

"Don't you go to preaching to me anymore," Dick called after him. "I'm wise to you."

Danny and Kay went out of the store and walked two or three blocks before Danny spoke. And when he did his voice was thick and edged with bitterness.

"What Dick said was true, Kay. I have been preaching one thing and doing another, so far as Tim is concerned."

"What do you mean?" she asked him.

"I've been wanting Tim to go to the Bible Institute with me, Kay," he said slowly, "so that he'd get good, sound teaching. But I've only been kidding myself when I said that was my only reason. I've been jealous of him. Terribly jealous. I didn't want him to go to Crestwood and get all that acclaim if I didn't."

There was a long, painful silence.

"That exhibition in the corner store a little while ago showed me just how far I've drifted from the Lord these past two or three weeks. I lost my temper in there because I knew in my heart that what they were saying was true," confessed Danny.

"It's happened now." Kay's voice was kind. "The question is, what can you do about it?"

He stopped short. "Would you mind going on home alone, Kay?" he said huskily. "I'm going back to the corner store."

When Danny went back into the building on the corner, Dick and his friends had just finished their malts and were getting their coats.

"I came back to tell you," Danny began doggedly, "that I'm sorry I lost my temper a few minutes ago."

The suddenness of his apology took the group by surprise. They stopped what they were doing and stared at him.

"The things you said about the way I've been treating Tim were true," he went on evenly. "I've been jealous of him, and I haven't acted as a Christian should. I'm going to make it right with Tim the first thing in the morning. I wanted you to know that."

The girl with Dick giggled a little, in embarrassment.

"I–I ought to be able to think of something funny to say," Dick mumbled.

"With the Lord's help," Danny concluded, "I'm going to make things right."

Nobody said anything more. The young people turned and went outside. Danny stood there for a moment or two, still trembling. It hadn't been easy to come back and apologize in front of the other kids, to admit that he had been wrong. It wouldn't be easy either to talk to Tim in the morning, but he knew that was what he would have to do.

CHAPTER 13

FRIENDS AGAIN

Danny Orlis overslept the following morning and didn't get to talk to Tim on the way to school. Between classes he looked for his friend, but Tim was nowhere to be seen. It wasn't until Danny went down to the gymnasium after school for the first indoor workout of the baseball squad that he saw him.

"Hi, Tim!" He tried to make his voice warm and friendly as Tim came out of the locker room and started over to the place where the coach was talking with a handful of the guys.

Tim Barton looked over toward him, scowled, and grunted disagreeably.

"All right!" Coach Collins shouted, calling the squad together. "We're going to start limbering up. You pitchers and catchers go over under the south goal and start playing catch."

Danny glanced at Tim. The young quarterback was also a catcher.

"You, Orlis," the coach called, "start throwing to Barton."

Danny and Tim stared at one another. Coach Collins had done it deliberately, Danny was sure of that.

In the tense silence that followed, Danny walked over to Tim. "I–I want to apologize to you, Tim," he began. "I've thought and said some things about you that I shouldn't have."

Tim scowled at him.

"You can stow that talk. It's not going to get any-where with me."

The practice was short. As soon as it was over, Danny took a shower and got quickly into his clothes. He planned on going directly to his room to study for an English exam, but Dick Bridges stopped him.

"I guess you guys can talk good religion," he said, laughing. "But when it comes to living it, you're just like the rest of us."

Danny stared as Dick swaggered down the corridor. He swallowed hard and bit his lower lip. After a moment or two he went down to his locker, got his coat and books, and waited for Tim just inside the front door.

Several guys walked past and spoke to him before Tim came down the hall, his head down, and his gaze boring into the floor.

"Hi, Tim!"

Tim looked up, his dark eyes snapping angrily. "I haven't got anything to say to you."

"What's the matter with us, Tim?" Danny asked.

"You know very well what's the matter," came the heated reply.

"I'm sorry for my part of the trouble between us. I want you to know that. I have no right to say anything about where you go to school, or why." Danny stopped for a moment and laid his hand on Tim's shoulder. "I don't want things to go on like this. I want to be friends with you, Tim."

"You had your chance," snarled Tim.

"We're both Christians, Tim," Danny continued. "I know that I've said some things about you that I shouldn't have said. And I'm sorry. Really, I am. If you feel that you want to go to Crestwood and play football, that's all right with me, fella. I'll have to admit that I've been jealous of you, and all the publicity you've gotten."

"You had the same chance as I did, Danny," Tim put in quickly. "If you'd just be smart enough to take it." He looked into his friend's eyes. "Why don't you change your mind, Danny? I know they'll still give you that scholarship if you'll take it. And just think of the fun we'd have."

"I've been thinking of the testimony that we're showing the gang here at school," Danny said in a subdued voice. "How many of them do you think are going to be interested in taking Christ as their Savior when they see how we're acting toward one another? Why, we aren't any different than the unsaved guys. Things haven't gone our way, so we've started to fight and bicker and talk about one another because of it. That's the way the world does, Tim."

Tim Barton straightened suddenly. For a moment, his eyes flashed with anger. And then the fire went out of them. He swallowed hard and moistened his lips.

"I know that, Danny," he said after a time. "And I feel as bad about it as you do. But you aren't the only one who did wrong. I've been the one who kept this quarrel going. You tried to clear things up, but I wouldn't let you."

The two boys stared at one another. Then Danny grinned and held out his hand. Tim took it and squeezed it happily. And a broad smile broke across his round face.

"Let's go in here and ask the Lord to forgive us too," he said, leading the way to an empty study hall.

"I've been miserable trying to stay mad at you, Danny," Tim confessed.

"I've been miserable about the whole affair too," said his friend.

After Danny and Tim had prayed together, they opened the schoolhouse door and walked down the sidewalk, arm in arm.

THE DANNY ORLIS SERIES

The Danny Orlis series, by Bernard Palmer, delivers a blend of adventure, mystery, and suspense through various settings—from the Canadian wilderness to Guatemalan jungles. Danny Orlis, an adept outdoorsman, skilled athlete, and committed Christian, employs his quick thinking, calm bravery, and biblical solutions to confront everyday problems and hair-raising dangers. Early stories focus on Danny navigating school life, sports, and outdoor challenges, while in later books, Danny and his wife Kay provide wisdom and guidance to youngsters facing lifelike situations and challenges. Having sold over two million copies, this series has made Palmer a renowned author in Christian youth literature. Palmer is also the author of the Felicia Cartright series and various other series for Christian youth.

AVAILABLE FROM WWW.ANEKOPRESS.COM